Superphonics® *Storybooks* will help your child to learn to read using Ruth Mis phonic method. Each story is been carefully written to incl and spellings.

The Storybooks are graded so your child can progress with confidence from easy words to harder ones. There are four levels - Blue (the easiest), Green, Purple and Turquoise (the hardest). Each level is linked to one of the core *Superphonics®Books*.

ISBN: 978 0 340 77352 9

Text copyright © 2001 Gill Munton
Illustrations copyright © 2001 Charlotte Hard

Editorial by Gill Munton
Design by Sarah Borny

The rights of Gill Munton and Charlotte Hard to be identified as the author and illustrator of this Work have been asserted by them in accordance with the Copyright, Designs and Patents Act 1988.

First published in Great Britain 2001

10 9 8 7 6 5 4 3

First published in 2001 by Hodder Children's Books, a division of Hachette Children's Books, 338 Euston Road, London NW1 3BH An Hachette UK Company. www.hachette.co.uk

Printed and bound in China by WKT Company Ltd.

A CIP record is registered by and held at the British Library.

Target words

This Purple Storybook focuses on the following sounds:

ee as in **tree** | **e-e** as in **these**
ea as in **bean** | **y** as in **hungry**

These target words are featured in the book:

asleep	sweet	leaned	here
been	sweetest	leaped	these
cheers	three	least	
cheese	tree	leave	angry
deed	weeds	leaves	happy
feeding		meal	happily
feet	beans	meat	hungry
free	beast	peace	hurry
greed	beaten	please	lazy
greedy	cream	pleased	nearly
green	dear	reached	really
keep	dream	reaches	shady
need	dreamed	screamed	silly
peeked	dreaming	seat	unhappy
peered	eat	steal	
see	eating	stealing	
seen	hear	treat	
sleep	heaved	wheat	
speed	leafy		

(Words containing sounds and spellings practised in the Blue and Green Storybooks and the other Purple Storybooks have been used in the story, too.)

Other words

Also included are some common words (e.g. **after**, **said**) which your child will be learning in his or her first few years at school.

A few other words have been used, to help the story to flow.

Reading the book

1 Make sure you and your child are sitting in a quiet, comfortable place.

2 Tell him or her a little about the story, without giving too much away:

Jack climbs the beanstalk to steal from the giant - but the second time, the giant has other ideas!

This will give your child a mental picture; having a context for a story makes it easier to read the words.

3 Read the target words (above) together. This will mean that you can both enjoy the story without having to spend too much time working out the words. Help your child to sound out each word (e.g. **t-r-ee**) before saying the whole word.

4 Let your child read the story aloud. Help him or her with any difficult words and discuss the story as you go along. Stop now and again to ask your child to predict what will happen next. This will help you to see whether he or she has understood what has happened so far.

Above all, enjoy the story, and praise your child's reading!

Ruth Miskin's
Superphonics ®
Purple Storybook

Jack and
the Beanstalk

by Gill Munton

Illustrated by Charlotte Hard

Hodder
Children's
Books

a division of Hachette Children's Books

Jack's mum was very unhappy.

Her hens just wanted to sleep,

and her cow was a lazy beast, too.

"What shall I do, Jack?" she wept.

"No eggs, no milk, no cheese, no meat,

No good sweet cream for a Sunday treat,

Nothing to drink, and nothing to eat -

Nothing to eat at all."

"At least you've got me!" said Jack.

"Let me go and sell the cow,

and then we can get some food."

On the way, Jack met a goblin.

"That's the sweetest face I ever did see!
Please will you give that cow to me?
And I'll give you these magic beans -
  one, two, three –
Three little magic beans!"

So Jack took the beans home to his mum.

"I really wish you hadn't come back.
You've made me very angry, Jack!
We could have had cheese,
  or wheat in a sack –
But a handful of silly BEANS?"

She threw the beans into a patch
of weeds.

When he went to sleep,

Jack dreamed about a leafy green plant.

And when he woke up, he saw that

his dream had come true!

"It's a beanstalk!" he said to himself.

"Those three beans really were magic!

I've never seen a TREE that high!

It nearly reaches to the sky!

And yes, I think I'm going to try

To climb to the very top!"

So Jack climbed up amid
the shady green leaves.

At the top, he saw a castle!
An Ogress was going in
with a plate of cheese.

"You look as if you need feeding up!"
she said to Jack.
"Would you like some cheese?"

"Yes, please!" said Jack.
"I am very hungry!"

But as he was eating, he could hear:

"Fee, fi, fo, fum!

I smell the blood of an Englishman!"

"Hurry, Jack, as fast as you can!"
Said the Ogress. "Hide in here!"

It was the Ogre!

"There's nobody here, dear!"
the Ogress said to him.
"You must have been dreaming!
Let's eat our meal in peace."

The greedy Ogre ate his meal.
Then he heaved a sack of gold
on to the seat.

"Look in the sack, count one, two, three,
Three lumps of gold,
  and they're all for me!
I'm as happy as ever an Ogre could be,
As long as I've got my GOLD."

Jack peeked out.

"I wish WE had some gold!"
he said to himself.
"When the Ogre is asleep,
I am going to steal some!"

"Now that I have done the deed,

I'm going home with all good speed,

I've beaten the Ogre and his greed,

I'm going home with my gold!"

Jack's mum was very pleased
with the gold.
So the next day, he climbed
the beanstalk again.

At the top, he saw the Ogress.
She was going into the castle
with a plate of meat.

"Have you come to steal
some more gold?" she said.

"No, said Jack,
"but I do need some meat.
I am very hungry!"

But as he was eating, he could hear:

"Fee, fi, fo, fum!

I smell the blood of an Englishman!"

"Hurry, Jack, as fast as you can!"
Said the Ogress. "Hide in here!"

It was the Ogre!

"There's nobody here, dear,"
the Ogress said to him.
"You must have been dreaming!
Let's eat our meal in peace."

The greedy Ogre ate his meal.
Then he leaned down
to pick up his golden harp.

"Play me some sweet songs,
   one, two, three,
Three songs from your golden strings,
   all for me!
I'm as happy as ever an Ogre could be,
As long as I've got my GOLD!"

Jack peered out.

"I wish WE had a golden harp!"
he said to himself.
"When the Ogre is asleep,
I am going to steal it!"

"Now that I have done the deed,

I'm going home with all good speed.

I've beaten the Ogre and his greed,

I'm going home with my gold!"

But the harp was still playing,
and it woke the Ogre up!

As Jack reached the top of the beanstalk,
the Ogre got to his feet!

"You have been stealing from me!"
he screamed.
"You will not leave here alive!"

"I've got to get away from this man!

Hurry, Mum, as fast as you can!

Fetch my axe, and hear my plan:

We'll chop the beanstalk down!"

Jack leaped down and reached for the axe.

He swung it at the beanstalk.

It crashed to the ground –

and so did the Ogre!

"That's the end of him!" said Jack.

"I am free, and we can keep all our gold!"

"Three cheers for Jack!" said Jack's mum.

And they lived happily ever after.